After Deat

Meredith Tucker © cor

I feel like I'm on a white page. What a strange sensation. I have no form only the ability to use language and remember who I am. I feel a wealth of confusion even though I know how I got here, but know myself – I am Jessica.

I allow the confusion to settle. It's amazing to know it's really worked. That I am here and that to exist forever might be possible. A beautiful valley of another world which I have seen before but always feared I wouldn't reach. I'm the type of person that worries about things.

I am dead. Yet science has come in waves and bounces since I was born in 2188. When I turned forty it all began. Thank God my parents were alive back then – the programme can be hard to swallow for spiritual people. I myself have always loved Jesus and have dedicated my heart and soul to being a Christian. Scientists don't yet know if a 'soul' goes onto to another life as well and whether this procedure effects that experience.

Yet scientists do know that the mind lives on and the person is the same as they were in life. They now exist in a special digital world, which is different in some ways from Earth – a version where all the dead since 2230 who choose to have their mind forever salvaged after their physical death will dwell.

I understand why very religious people choose to pass away the normal way. Yet neither my mum or dad were one of them, so when they died, weeks later I was able to talk to them on Watts-app and Facebook.

I don't know how long I've been dead. Yet when you sign the contract to go into 'Second Life', as it is called globally, you're informed about what the experience is like.

I'll explain all that but I want to dwell in the moment that is now, on the white page I knew about but can hardly explain coherently.

I see some lights on the white and writing forms in the blank. 'Welcome to Second Life' it says.

I'm here, I think and I hear myself say the words in the voice of myself as an elderly woman.

"Yes, welcome to Second Life. My name is Dr Brian Messing. You selected me as the general psychologist to help you through your period of adjustment on Second Life." His voice is clear and calm.

I feel giddy at the idea I've already connected to this part of the process. I thought it would be slower, but no, here I am, talking to the man that will guide me through my death.

"All treatment through this process is provided by the NHS, providing excellent healthcare in life and on the second phase," Dr Messing informs me.

"When will I take form? All I feel is audio and a whiteness around me," I ask.

"Soon, Jessica. We need to assess the level of your mood before that process is inserted into your key programming. You are still you, feel the wholeness of your mind and it will happen a lot quicker."

I remember my dad took two weeks before he was online. It was so lovely to hear from him on Watts-app. He said how he felt happy and had bought a digital house. You can either have one state assigned or buy a fancier one for a pittance in comparison to the cost of homes in the physical world.

He was reasonably comfortable in his life and had left me a good home in London when he died. I remember I was forty-eight when he passed away. He had been a good dad and knowing he would forever be in my life made it so much easier to deal with the emotions of him passing on.

I often went to church and prayed for the spirits of pets and grandparents who were around before this scientific breakthrough. God didn't have to be separate from science. Belief in God remained in the digital world. Love of God is eternal.

"I'm thinking about a lot of things," I say to Dr Messing. I've never met him but remember seeing his picture and information on the large folder of psychologists. The NHS had contacted me and I was to pick one to work for me, as I was getting old and frail.

If you die unexpectedly and have opted for the 'Second Life' service, your psychologist is picked for you. They are people alive on Earth working within the digital program.

"How are you feeling?" Dr Messing asks.

"How long have I been in this new state for?"

"We will get to that in just a moment. First you need to describe your feelings to me," he says.

"I feel OK. I can't remember everything about how I died. It's like a blur in my mind but I know everything else. I know who I am… I'm Jessica Page. I know what my life was like and now that I'm here, I've obviously died. I feel a bit nervous because all I'm sensing is the colour white around me and our voices. Yet, I was told it would be like this at first so that's helping me not to panic."

"That's good. It's good to express feelings at this part of the process. It allows you to acclimatize to the unique state of being you are entering. Now I want you to tell me about yourself. As you do you might experience a buzzing, this is part of your senses awakening in this new second phase digital world, which will feel as real to you as on Earth."

I've seen the adverts on TV, with the digitized images of deceased people as full and vivid as if they never died; yet they're in the digital world. They look old at first and then seem to slip back into an adult age they were comfortable in. Unless the person dies young and then they're allowed to grow older in appearance as their mind matures.

When my dad died, he looked elderly on the digitize channel on my TV at first. Talking to me from beyond the grave, he was happy. He showed me the house he had bought in the second phase world. It was a farm with land. It would have cost at least half a million in reality, but there it cost around the equivalent of five pounds.

Like I said, he had left me a flat in London. I was a mother of three when he died and had my own home in Buckinghamshire. I had a life as a teaching assistant. So, we just rented out his home when he passed away. I remember him being pleased with this. He made me promise to use the money from the rent to pay off my mortgage as quickly as I could.

He died of old age at eighty-three. He'd had a hard life but was a good-hearted person who lived a life I would describe as kindly.

When I came to his flat the day after his passing, I remember packing most of his things to go to the charity shop. I kept all of his paintings and photos and some ornaments. I wanted to donate the remainder of his belongings to charity; I didn't have space in my home for another's belongings. I took a couple of snaps on my phone, and felt a sense of being okay with the moment.

"My mind is thinking about my dad's death and how he and my mum both entered second phase. I wish my grandmother had been around when the scientific breakthrough was made," I say to Dr Messing.

"Thinking about loved ones in the second phase world is natural. You would have been able to commune with them via social media and computers, but now you'll see them face to face. I know how sad it can be when we have loved ones who didn't get to experience this. The notes that I have about you, say you're a woman of Christian faith. Does this help you with these feelings?"

"Yes," I say without having to think about it. "I believe there is something for the soul. I wonder if being here affects that. I don't know but I couldn't risk missing out on this for something that may not even be. Even though I had faith, I also believe firmly in science. I've got an anthropology degree, you know."

"Yes, that's on your file. No one can know what lies beyond and if a soul exists. Maybe one day science and other fields of research will understand this spiritual question more deeply," Brian said.

"Yes, I'm sure they will."

I feel a sensation of buzzing and I lock onto the sense of texture, which seems to be becoming part of the experience. I hold onto it as it shakes a sense of fabric to what was, before, just me talking in mist of whiteness.

"Your readings state you're starting to materialize in second phase. Just do your best to relax while this happens. Let's talk more as this will help the process," Brian says in a calming voice.

"I remember when I saw my dad on the TV channel where we would connect with people in second phase. He looked the same as he had before he died. He looked full of life at the same time. I remember how that was a beautiful sight to behold," I told him.

"I'm feeling dizzy," I tell Brian suddenly. The buzzing is quieter now.

"That's all normal. You're taking form in the digital world. Do you want to talk more or shall I explain to you what's happening and guide you through the process? Whatever you feel is best, Jessica."

"Talk me through it, tell me things."

"Your body is becoming whole with digital tissue. You belong to a world where your data is being uploaded now that your consciousness is working. You've been dead a day. Your microchip has been successfully installed onto the great data readers and backup chips are safely stored in vaults around the world. You are becoming part of second phase," Brian says.

I know all this from the day course everyone takes who signs up to enter second phase. I am excited to think it's happening to me. It will be weird viewing my children through digi-view, a program which allows you to see them through a hologram room that gives the feeling of being in the same space.

I feel myself and can see colours swirling in the white. I see a big blur and realize it's the shape of my arms and legs. As I focus on the image it becomes more concrete and the black blur takes colour and form, turning into limbs.

It happens quickly the next sensation and I feel is a sharp ping in my ears. I am fully myself now.

"Welcome to second phase," Dr Brian Messing says.

The white has evaporated into a brown room and I am standing in the office. The office all second phase users will meet when they 'form' is described in the leaflet you're given in life.

Dr Messing is sitting on a chair behind a table on which sits a picture of a dog. I am standing in a room containing brown furniture and magnolia walls. I feel good, knowing I'm here and formed, ready to take the next step.

Chapter 2

Dr Brian Messing looks like the photo I remember from the folder, when I chose him to be my psychologist. I remember that he has a PhD in Psychology from the University of Bristol. He is a tall man with short brown hair and kindly eyes.

"It's good to see you," I say.

"Yes, you too, Jessica."

"I don't remember my death yet."

"You will as time goes by. Some people who enter second phase remember it instantly. Let me check your criteria and see if I'm legally allowed to tell you how you died."

"Sure."

Dr Brian types on his thin laptop. He is not really in second phase as he isn't dead. He's connected by visual holographic images which make him look as if he's here, but he has no physical presence.

All electronic devices such as laptops are made of a similar digital tissue, which allows me to be physical in a digital world. It's basically a digital dimension.

"Yes, we're in luck. You requested that you be informed of your death and other Earthly matters such as the organising of your funeral and family inheritance from your estate." He narrows his eyes as he types on the computer. "It says that you died in your sleep. Your second phase chip kicked in and the coroner was noticed of your death at 9 pm on the 28 August 2280."

"Ninety is a good age to die," I say with a smile.

"It is indeed, Jessica. You've been here three days. Your family have been notified and informed of your progression to second phase. Your estate has not yet been dealt with and, as you requested, your eldest daughter Eliza will be dealing with your funeral which will take place early September. As requested, no digital guests from second phase will be attending as the funeral will be just for the living to pay their respects."

"That's the way I wanted things. I'm really pleased."

I had left property to each of my daughters. I left my eldest daughter Eliza the flat in Harrow, which my father had given to me. I left Kate the house in Buckinghamshire my mother had left me and my youngest Miranda would inherit the house I had bought myself with the help of my parents.

My husband and I had been very independent financially. He was the same age as me but still alive. We lived in his house and rented mine out. It was a little bungalow in Chesham, which he had bought in his forties.

When I was ready to talk to my family, I'd see what Miranda wanted to do regarding the tenants. They still had two years left on their lease.

"Would you like to see what you look like?" Dr Messing asked me.

"Yes."

He opened his desk drawer, took out a mirror and passed it to me.

I remembered my old wrinkly face with affection. Even in old age I was a pretty woman. I'd always loved my brown hair that grew so very long. In old age when my hair became grey, I would dye it dark brown.

I was wearing the glasses I remember putting on the side table before going to sleep. It hit me that I recalled going to bed that night. Getting into the comfortable king-sized bed that Casper and I share. I was tired and glad of my bed. That was it, but that's all the memory consisted of. It was rather beautiful to think that had been my last moments in the real world. Falling asleep with Casper's last words to me being, "Good night, dear."

I was wearing the allocated black trousers and black t-shirt that I selected from the catalogue to be the outfit that I would enter second phase in.

"How are you feeling, Jessica?" Dr Messing smiled warmly.

"I feel good. I'm a little giddy with excitement. I obviously didn't want to die, I'd have liked to made it to one hundred, but I'm glad to be conscious and solid. I feel good and blessed."

"You're doing great and making brilliant progress in second phase. I'm happy that your adjustment is going smoothly. I will write up my report and sign off. A guide will shortly connect. They will show you into your desired living quarters and take you through the finances of your first second phase home. I'll stay with you until he or she connects in."

Brian took out his mobile phone and called for a guide to connect. He smiled and looked content. I've heard how working in second phase was great pay.

Second phase is a universal function all around the world for any person who opts for it. Since the dawn of second phase, all world countries have had some sort of national health service whether it's very basic or as advanced as our long-standing NHS.

You can choose private health care in second phase or to be cared for via the health care service of your country of citizenship. Although comfortably off, I didn't want private health care as I feel you need to be richer than I to justify it. So I was more than happy to use the NHS.

The guide connected into the room, appearing as if by magic. She was a young woman in her early twenties with mid-length pink hair. She was pretty wearing frosty pink lipstick and a dress that ended just above her slender knees.

"Hi, I'm Emily," she said.

"Well now that your guide is here, I'll be signing off. I'll speak again with you soon, Jessica. It was a pleasure to meet you and be assigned to your case."

"Thank you, Dr Brian. It's been great to meet you," I say.

"Until next session," he says and before I know it he has disappeared as if he was never there. His laptop flashes green as it downloads all the data into his physical copy in the real world.

"Right," Emily says, "let's take you around the plaza where I can give you a tour of some of second phase.

You're fully solid and ready to enjoy the wonderful attractions of this new and exciting world."

Chapter 3

Emily hands me a replica of the phone that lay by my bedside table the night I died – an android device of the highest calibre. It allows one to call and text people in the real world as well as in second phase.

I go to take the phone from her and my hand goes through Emily's immaterial hand. She smiles as I take the device, my hands slightly shaking.

"It's weird getting used to the fact that us workers are not actually part of the second phase world," she acknowledges with a smile.

"Yes, quite," I say as I turn on the phone – all my data is on it. The picture of our little West-highland terrier Snowball is on the home screen. I'll miss being able to cuddle her.

Emily then hands me my wrist-watch, a type only available in second phase. I've read about these in the leaflet, how they allow you to travel to any destination in this world. You just need the IP address which you can save into your watch for ease of access.

"Right, let me help you get to the plaza, where we can talk finances and what sort of home you want to live in," Emily says.

"The address of the plaza is simply 'Plaza'. It's a main hub for all second phase workers and residents to mingle and shop. It is well known for 'newbie' residents as a hot stop for getting great deals on accessories you'll need, like a bag to put your phone – of course, don't worry if you misplace it, no one can steal it as it's connected to your central data. All you have to do is pick a retrieval word and it will return to your hand."

"I remember hearing about that," I say.

"We've set the pre-installed retrieval word as 'find me', it's attuned to your programming and data so no one else saying this word can access your phone."

"Let's just leave it at that word for now then," I say.

"For now, the only address in your watch is the Plaza. Just click on it and say 'Plaza' but make sure are watches are touching so we both get there together!"

I turn on my watch, it beeps and a bright blue screen welcomes me. Emily comes towards me and our watches touch. I say "Plaza" and in a blink of an eye, we are in a grand outdoor shopping centre.

"Well done. You're doing so well, Jessica. This is the plaza, one of my favourite shopping centres in second phase".

"How many shopping centres are there here?"

"Well, the population of deceased people who are reborn in second phase are over the living population of Earth! Imagine that, these people need fulfilment and shops to occupy them. As the population of this world grows, more cities and expansion packs are programmed to house the population." Emily's smile is that of a bright confident woman.

"It's so amazing." I look around at the open space. The sky is a mesmerizing pink.

We are surrounded by shops that look smartly kept. Some of the names I recognize from the real world.

I see an elderly man walking with what I imagine is a guide like Emily, as she is showing him around. They are speaking in what sounds like Mandarin. His guide is pointing to the shops and sculptures that decorate the shopping centre.

There are trees carefully pruned in pots. Everything looks so well kept.

"Are most of the workers from the real world?" I ask.

"It's about half and half," Emily tells me. "What sort of food do you like? Maybe we could order your first meal in second phase. You'll be amazed how it tastes the same as food did on Earth, or so I'm told."

"I... I don't want food just yet. Maybe a coffee."

"Fine. Let me take you to a Starbucks?" she offers.

I follow her as she walks to the nearest Starbucks. The big green display of the well-known chain is welcoming amongst the new. We enter and it's absolutely huge. It's moderately packed.

"Let me show you a cool trick on the watch." Emily beams. "In Starbucks number 33 of Plaza, turn off sound of conversations around me and my client Jessica Page." The watch makes a series of little beeps and all the speech around us is silenced. "They're still talking but this will allow us to have some peace and privacy," Emily explains.

Emily buys me a coffee. I sit down on the comfortable seats and look at the people around her while she queues. There're a lot of young people who are very beautiful. You can enhance your appearance in second phase without the pain of plastic surgery, so maybe they are people who desired to do this.

Emily returns with my coffee. I look at the big white mug and take it to my lips. It's nicely hot and the strong taste is just like how I remember it, rich and warm. It makes me smile because it's another part of this whole experience that makes it feel like I'm not dead at all!

"Good?" Emily smiles.

"Just the way Starbucks tastes at home."

"I love Starbucks. So, you lived in Chesham Buckinghamshire?" she asks.

"Yeah, I lived there with my husband."

"Well I don't know if you remember from your day course but every town in the world has a printed version in second phase that marks exactly the same shops and buildings that were there. Every ten years another copy is made so people can choose the decade of a place, if they wish to live in part of the printed world, as it's called in second phase."

"Where do you live in the real world, Emily?" I ask.

"I'm from Manchester. But I just finished uni in Bath, just went back home recently and have been working for second phase since I moved home."

"That's great. What did you study at university?"

"I studied sociology," she says.

"That's great. I studied anthropology for my degree," I say. "I was twenty-six when I graduated."

"Amazing, Jessica. Where did you study?"

"University of East London." My coffee tastes great and I notice I've already finished it.

"Would you like another one? It's on me!"

"No, thanks. I'd usually have to worry about my bladder, but that's not an issue now, is it?"

"Yeah, it's no longer an issue. No need for peeing. Your body will still feel full if you over eat or drink. You can get drunk if you want or you can alter your alcohol-resistance settings at the doctors'. Everything here is so cool!"

"I'm not much of a drinker, so I won't be getting drunk often." I smile at her, enjoying our conversation.

"Right, Jessica. Shall we sort you out with a home? I've been in your company one hour and my shift has seven hours left so we've plenty of time."

"Yes, how does that all work?" I ask.

She takes out a thin tablet from her back-pack and shows me an app called 'Second home'. The app has a picture of a little house on it. She clicks on the app and types quickly.

"Okay, I've just put in your user name and it says you allocated yourself ten thousand British pounds towards your second phase fund. Money works differently here, as you will be aware. Second-phase is an ultra-micro economy."

"God!" I sit back and laugh to myself. "I remember my dad telling me he bought a house with a farm for what would be worth five pounds in English money."

"Yes, property really hasn't got the same value here in second phase. You can't make money on property and you cannot get money for a property you sell, so really it's very different."

"Well I know you can live in a free home in second phase, but as I've so much currency and property is so cheap, I'd like to look into somewhere nice. I'm not into opulent homes so I won't be buying a mansion or anything like that."

"Cool! Well you can always move if you get bored of it. Just remember however much it cost you don't get back as you can't sell property the same way as you do on Earth. It's one of the ways the programmers help fund this technology."

"That's fair enough," I say. "Especially considering there is free accommodation for all here as well as state benefits."

"Exactly!" Emily beams. "Do you think you'd want to live in a printed town or city, or would you like to explore some of the designed worlds of second phase?"

I think about the question. I have friends that live on a replica of Mars here in second phase and other people who have stayed with what's normal, in a printed town of their home.

"When was the last print out of Chesham?" I ask.

She types on her tablet. "2270, the next print out is due 2280 in six months from now."

"Is my house for sale in the latest print out, or even the one of 2260, the house I bought myself I mean, or even the house Casper owns if I'm allowed to buy the print out of that?"

She types in her tablet again. "It's available on every print out. Your homes have never been purchased on the print out. Do you want to move into somewhere familiar?"

I remember taking the photos for the town's print outs. It was so simple, I just moved their special digital camera around each room and it scanned it into their computer systems.

"I'd like to move into my own home, the one I bought when I was in my mid-thirties. The home I left my youngest, Miranda."

Emily types on her tablet. She turns it around to me and shows me pictures of the house from 2070 when the photographs were taken. Tenants have been living there since Casper bought his own home in the same town.

I let the tenants decorate it how they pleased. They were a young family who had painted the three-bedroom house pinks and yellows. It was very tidy when the photos were taken for the print out.

"How much is it?" I say, curious to think. I paid £240,000 pounds for it.

"Not much here in the print out for 2270, its digi currency translates to two pounds and fifty-five pence.

"Brilliant. Well as I put ten grand aside for my second phase, I'll definitely take it."

"Okay. Well you can buy it here on the tablet if you like?" She opens her back-pack again and removes a folder.

"Here are your things that you'll need. Your passport and a bank card. Your death and birth certificate are there too."

I take the bank card out. I opened a bank account when I became elderly and frail. I had saved ten thousand pounds for this day, all the rest of the money would be for Casper, as I felt leaving my children a home each was enough. I'd given my grandchildren what I could in my will.

The bank card has my name on it and my signature on the back from when I opened it in the real world. It's got the ten thousand, which translates into a lot of digi currency.

"So, you're sure this is the home you want to get? You can always buy somewhere else another time and move out."

"In this experience right now, I think it's what I'd like. It will be nice to redecorate it to how we had it when the children were young. So, when I see their holograms, it will feel like nothing has changed."

"That's really lovely." Emily smiles. "Shall we pay for it then? Final answer?"

"Final decision. One hundred percent the house I want," I say.

Emily instructs me that all I need to do is touch the 'pay here' application on the page for my house on the print out, and it's mine. I touch the payment and it flashes green, a few beeps emitting from the tablet.

"Your new home is bought. The address will simply be 'home' on your watch. You can print some keys for anyone in second phase who might want to stay with you at times, like your dad or mum."

"Soon, maybe," I say.

"Do you want to go home now and settle in? I've got plenty of time on my shift so I can help you."

"Have you got time on your shift to go exploring?"

"Of course. Let me check the time. Six hours left. How about we do three hours of exploring and then I can take you home. You'll be able to watch the manual at home so if you need any more assistance you can call any one of the helplines available and speak to real people able to show you how to get around second phase."

"I've always been good with technology and gadgets. So I think that will be fine. Yes, let's go exploring for three hours and then we can go home and I'll get settled in."

I ask her to order me another drink – decaf tea this time. I ask Emily about talking to my family. I feel unsure texting them. She shows me how to turn my phone contacts on from Earth. I do so and see that my facebook has turned green, which means the person has died but is in second phase.

My hundred and forty contacts consist of other dead people as well as living family and friends. There are lovely messages on my wall. I see messages from friends and family and it makes me well up with tears.

"You okay?" Emily asks.

"It's just rather a lot to take in. Do you know how many days I've been in second phase for?"

She checks on her tablet. "Three, it's not been long."

I like some of the messages and write a message to my friends and family on my wall.

'Safely in second phase. I died aged ninety. I was born on the 22 July 2190 and had a wonderful life. Life is hard but glorious. Please opt for second phase on your preferences if that is your so desire as I can tell you already it is magical. I'm sitting in Starbucks with a guide ordering a coffee and I can taste it. I will call and text you all when I'm a little more adjusted. I've moved into my old house that I lived in near Emmanuel Church. I love you all. I've been told by the staff working here that I've only been here three days. Thank you for all the lovely messages and wall posts. I'll get back to you all soon.'

Chapter 4

Emily shows me images of some of the worlds within second phase. Earth is just one of them but the others are made up planets. You can live on planets within our solar system as the digital versions are habitable! NASA took scans of their landscape and architects in second phase did the rest to make amazing worlds based on Mars, Saturn and Jupiter as well as other planets in our galaxy.

I wasn't feeling adventurous enough to visit a digital moon, but I was curious about the other worlds. Emily showed me one that I liked the sound of called Lexi. It had been designed by an American and was a planet where one had to be welcoming of equal marriage rights for all. You had to be accepting of gay and lesbian people as well as the trans community. You had to sign a form that said you were of left-wing ideology politically and must have never run in any right wing political rallies or parties.

I had voted either liberal democrat or labour all my life, so I was intrigued to visit this planet. Emily explained it had over 130 large cities in the twenty countries that made up Lexi. None of them were based on Earth as it was frowned upon to model planets on Earth.

Anyone could create a planet in second phase providing they got over ten million validated signatures from people who were to join second phase when they died. It was part of the bureaucracies of second phase, but I feel it was fair as it takes a lot of programming and money to develop.

I told Emily I just wanted to visit somewhere that was cool today. A quiet town within one of the countries of Lexi, where I could maybe sing some karaoke. I really wanted to express myself, as singing was something I always adored in life.

Not only could you watch the Voice for all the countries in the real world, but there was a version for second phase singers. It aired on a channel for arts and entertainment created by the people who lived here.

If you became famous on second phase your verified twitter would hold a green tick instead of the blue tick.

I was in the mood for a little karaoke and maybe even a drop of socializing. Emily typed information into her search engine of Lexi. Half the world would be in night time now on the planet. She told me about a town called Nilba in a country called Freedom. She told me it was a welcoming town with a lot of people she thought seemed likeminded to me. Apparently, there were two great recording studios in Nilba and people on Earth would often record albums using their hologram as they paid a lot less to produce the music.

We decided that Nilba sounded like a great town to visit. Emily informed me the town had a population of 70,000 second phase residents and a population of workers and visitors from Earth in their hologram form.

Before we went to Nilba, Emily advised I change my look. We went to French connection where I bought a bag and coat. The coat was a sophisticated blue number and I felt it make me look cared for, which is a nice thing to see on an old lady.

When I rejuvenate to youth through the doctors' visits I'm to have, I thought I'd keep this coat for when I'm ready to have a stab at my twenties. I wasn't sure yet if I wanted to stay looking ninety until I saw Casper in this world, or if I wanted to look younger.

I got a nice dress that was a bit of an old lady dress, but after all that's what I was still. I wore sensible flat shoes to complete the outfit.

We put our watches together and a minute later we were in Nilba. It was a tropical seaside town. The weather was calm and as we walked around together, I took my coat off. Emily offered to hold it – even though she had no form, she was able to hold items in this world which seemed weird, but it was all part of the amazing science that gave me this life.

We got food before Karaoke. It was only seven in the evening in this world's time zone. I got a vegetarian burrito and a cup of tea.

After the food I checked my phone. Casper had sent a sweet message about how he would miss me even though he would see me again. He sent me a photograph of

Snowball our dog. She looked happy and bright in the picture with a red ball in her mouth.

I replied to his text. *It's all overwhelming. I've been here three days. But it's great. I'm happy. I bought a home in a print out of Chesham, the same house I'm leaving Miranda.*

He typed back before I had a chance to put my phone away.

The same house. Amazing. You're OK? I love you.

I replied, telling him that I was going on my first adventure. I took a snap of the town of Nilba and told him how it was in a world called Lexi. I told him I was going to sing karaoke. He requested that I record it and send it to him.

Emily was happy to record for me while I sung. So we entered a quiet karaoke bar that was also an Irish themed pub. The bartender was a stocky woman with brown hair who greeted me with a calm smile.

The karaoke was to start shortly and a handful of people were there. I requested to sing a Micheal Smith song. I told them I was new to second phase and we'd need to get back to my home soon, as this was my first trip with my guide.

"What are your names?" asked the DJ.

"I'm Jessica and my guide is Emily."

"Well I hope you enjoy it here. Does your guide want to sing as well?"

"Well part of my job is helping people assimilate into this world, so sure, I'll sing too."

I ordered a half pint of cola. Popcorn was placed on the table for free, but I was too nervous to nibble on food; I was here to sing. I wanted to see how I sounded now because I'd had a good a voice in my life.

I'd had five singing teachers in my life, four female and one male. I had adored singing. I'd been in a rock band when I was seventeen and done karaoke whenever I could throughout my life.

The first woman who sung looked in her thirties with perfectly bleached white hair. She was pale and slender. She didn't look advanced by Second Life but just normally pretty, which I thought was nice. She sung a modern pop song. When she was finished everyone cheered and clapped.

"Welcome to the stage a new visitor to the Fladh," the DJ announced. "Everyone give a round of applause for Jessica."

I handed Emily my phone and told her to video my performance and send it to Casper.

I felt butterflies dance in my stomach as I stepped onto the stage. I sang a song I had really liked in my late twenties called, 'I Am Here' by Michael Smith.

The microphone made the acoustics sound great and I felt so good singing. My voice sounded like an old woman's, but an old woman who was me, one who could sing well! I felt good and the adrenalin was powerful.

When the song ended, I sat back down and we sent the video to Casper. As he watched it Emily excitedly complimented me on my voice. I told her a little about how I really loved singing.

I drowned my coke and begun to nibble on the popcorn. I knew we didn't have all the time in the world to sing tonight. Also I wanted to go home at some point and get to grips with my new home. I knew I had assigned one computer for the second phase move.

I had my mobile and a tablet also. I had donated old computers to a science library, which deals with using your data to understand people of the past. Yet all my digital data was still mine. Old computers would be researched, analysing my web activity and documents by historians.

Emily sang a song I hadn't heard before but her voice was pleasant enough. She had a nice soft voice and the song suited that. When she finished, she received a round of applause.

I told her I wanted to go and have a look around Nilba for a while, before going to my new home.

"Some good singing there, girls," said the DJ. "Will you be coming back again?"

"Certainly" I promised.

It was around eight thirty in the evening when we left the pub. More people were entering the venue and I was glad that we had sung when it was quieter.

"How are we doing for time?" I ask.

"We've still got an hour on our schedule before I want to take you home."

So we walked together around the beachy town. I bought Casper a teddy bear wearing a Nilba sweater and gave his email address so that he would be able to print it out on his 3D printer at home.

Casper had replied on Watt's-app. *You've still got it, what a great singer you always were and will be.*

We walked near the sea that seemed to stretch for miles. People were surfing and swimming in a water they simply couldn't drown in. There were no sharks or jelly-fish to worry about!

"Do you have many clients, Emily?" I asked.

"Yeah. I work six days a week. So I'm working with six people who are new to second phase. That's my job."

"You started after uni, right?"

"Yeah, I moved back to Manchester to live with my mum and save for a house. The pay's quite good in second phase."

"It's an interesting job, I imagine. I think when I was your age, I would have found it interesting and enjoyable too."

I take some more photos and send them to Casper. I see there are messages on my phone from my children and people who are also dead like mum and dad. I send them a quick *I'm OK. I'll talk to you on the phone soon* and send them the video of me singing karaoke. I feel it's something happy to send them.

I upload some of the photographs on my Instagram. I have three accounts and one is where I only follow celebrities and interesting people. I see that my accounts have gone green to indicate I'm on second phase. I don't read any likes or comments but simply upload the lovely photographs of Nilba.

We place our watches together and within a moment I'm back outside the printed version of my house – my new home.

It's late at night on Earth and the time in the printed world of second phase always mirrors this. I look at my watch and the time has changed to 1 a.m.

"You can just open the door, there's no need for a key, only you can decide who comes in," Emily says.

I open the door and invite Emily in. The house is decorated the way it was when the photos for the 2270 print of Chesham were taken. I actually remember that as I had to reschedule my week to make sure I got them done.

All the pictures of the tenants' family had been taken down when the print was taken so it looks like my home. The furniture isn't my style and the sofa is far too plain. I remember I kept hideous flowery sofas that I loved in this house for years when the children were growing up. I had bought them from a charity shop.

"There's a fridge but there won't be any food in the house. You can order a takeaway or go to the supermarket tonight. Your laptop and tablet are downloaded and in the front room table. Just like your phone they'll be the way they were when you set them in preparation for second phase. You can even download food from an app," Emily informs me.

"Yes, I remember all this from the day courses and adverts on TV. I'll write a few emails to my family later."

I sit down on the black leather couch. There is no TV where one should be. I'll order one online later to be downloaded into my front room.

I take a few photographs of the house and text Casper who is still awake as he's showing as online. I send him the photos and tell him to get some rest.

He says he's finding it hard to sleep the last few nights. I tell him to take an Ovaltine drink and do some art work until he feels rested.

I'm glad that people know I'm okay but I'm finding it hard to deal with it all. I'm happy and pleased to be here but it's a lot to adjust to. Emily tells me how to cut noise from neighbours through my settings. I do this and adjust for animal settings – there are no birds in this world but the animations create auditory noises for people, so you feel more at home.

Animals can't enter second phase as it is against the law in all countries to bring an animal to live a second life that they wouldn't understand.

"Two hours left." Emily smiles. "I'll be back next week on the same day."

"What day is it?"

"Tuesday. Three days since you entered second phase."

I decide to order a takeaway. The food is brought to us by a robot and as we have already payed when ordering it, he thanks us and leaves after delivering it.

I know you can just download food from the Food app but I like the nostalgia of a food delivery robot. I remember them fondly from life on Earth.

I eat my vegetarian pizza and drink my pepsi. I ask Emily if she has my number and she explains that I already have her work phone number.

I look in my phone and there it is under a contact list of second phase associates. Not only do I also have Brian Messing's email contacts, but I have lots of helplines already listed on my phone.

Emily tells me about her studies at Bath in sociology, how she had her heart hurt on the final year. She describes her failed relationship at university which really affected her self-esteem. How it felt like the best thing to move back to Manchester where she could be with her family.

She hands over my folder with my passport and other things that I needed and asks me to sign a form stating I was happy for her to continue to be my guide. I did so and then the session was closed off a little early.

She waves goodbye to me before signing off and disappearing. I was in my house alone. I look around the clean and welcoming home and think about how I would hire a decorating robot to revamp it in some way. I'd have more granny-ish furniture that had been my style since my twenties. I guess I felt it made a home homely and comfortable.

I'd only eaten one slice of the pizza. I knew food was just accessible by downloading it on my tablet here in this digital world.

I decide to turn off the lights and go to bed. The unused bed is fresh and smells of perfect cleanliness. It is warm and comfortable. As I lay in bed with just the night light on for a moment, I take my glasses off and found my eyesight was better than I recalled.

I say a quick prayer in my mind to God, thanking him for science and the family I love in this second phase world who had died before me, and the people back on Earth. I prayed for those who died before my forties, such as my great grandmother, who were on the true other side. I like to believe there is a God, and that they will have consciousness too and be able to feel the presence of my love in a prayer from this digital world.

Chapter 5

I sleep well. My subconscious is doing backflips and my dreams are fragmented, yet I don't feel any cryptic messages from beyond the grave.

I look at my phone and smile at the thought that I won't need to charge it now I'm in second phase. It's 10 a.m.

I note how I haven't felt the desire to use the toilet in this realm. I guess it's not required when you're not real in the same way as you were before.

I put on the outfit I was wearing yesterday. I'll have to get some more clothes in town today.

I leave my house and walk to town. There are cars on the road, which is surreal. Not many but one or two. People walk by me and smile. I walk past the first church at the traffic lights and then down the long road that leads into town. Past all the houses and little independent shops. It's like I never died.

When I get inside Cafe Nero it looks just as it does in the real world. The photos were taken nine years ago for this print out but nothing much has changed inside. I walk to the front and order a slice of chocolate cake and tea. The man who serves me has spikey blond hair and looks in his mid-twenties.

There is a couple sitting in the cafe which is nice. I almost want to try and strike up a conversation, but feel the regular constraints holding me back. I need to pick a conversation with a stranger at an art class or something like that, where it's more formal to do so.

As I sip my tea, I get my phone out and take a picture of my food to send to Casper. He's not online, so I guess he's asleep.

I start going through my facebook posts on my wall. I reply to a few from friends and family telling me things like 'Rest in peace', and 'see you on the second side'.

Some people from church have passed away naturally because they don't believe in second phase. Thankfully all my close friends from church opted for this world. I understand where those who opt out of this come from. Real life is a lot. It was enough for people before 2230.

Luckily second phase hasn't caused any wars in the world. I suspect it's because people don't want to lose the right to enter it. They want the conscious world it brings to them even when they are no longer alive.

Murderers and people of other terrible crimes lose their right to enter second phase. We do not have the death penalty in England, so these people simply don't get to carry on living.

Criminals of smaller crimes are permitted to enter second phase which I think is fair enough. I don't think you should lose your right unless your crime takes away all your humanity.

I look at the texts from the girls. Eliza has joked wishing me happy death day. She has sent me some photographs from her day and told me how the family are managing. We chat on Watts-app as I sip my tea. I describe to her what it's like and how I'm eating chocolate cake.

She says how she misses me and would like to see me via the hologram soon. I say I'll try and call her up later or tomorrow as I'm just getting my bearings.

I text my dad who would have heard the news that I've died as will mum. They're both in this realm.

My dad calls me after I send him a few texts. I haven't been great with my phone considering all the messages I've had since I died.

"Hi," he says. He sounds healthy and void of any health ailments he ever had in life.

"I'm in second phase, finally," I say. "Ninety's a good age."

"Older than I managed," my dad tells me. This place is great. Have you got a home yet?"

"Yes. I've moved into the home I left to Miranda from the print out. Um, can I come and visit you? Will you text me your address so I can get there by my watch?"

"Sure of course. I'll text that to you now. When are you coming over?"

"I'll pop round now."

"Okay, see ya soon." Dad hangs up.

He texts me the address of his house in Hemel Hemstead. I look at the address. I've seen the pictures from his phone and when we've talked by hologram, but now I'll be walking around his house. It will be like when I used to visit him in London when we were alive.

*

I type in the address via the holographic keypad that I draw up on my watch. Moments passed and there I am standing outside the entrance of my father's farm. The gates are high and it's located in a village just near Hemel Hemstead. He also lives in the printed world of second phase.

The scenery is beautiful. I open the black gates and enter a front garden full of pretty flowers. A statue of a pig is sitting by the door. I knock and wait.

Dad opens the door. He died at eighty-three but he's younger now through the rejuvenation procedure. He looks about forty, his hair is no longer grey and his pot-belly is gone.

"Come on in," he says.

I follow him into the house. The hall walls are white with paintings colouring the wall. He leads me to a large sitting room.

"Cup of tea?" he asks me.

"Yes please," I say as I sit on the sofa in front of the large television.

While dad brews the tea I look around. I recognize some of the paintings on the wall as his style. He's done a self-portrait. There are photographs of dogs we've had in our life such as Sasha and Misty. The pictures are from when we took them to the park on Christmas day. It was my second year of university, so I remember it clearly as a landmark in my life.

Dad returns with the mugs of tea. "Settling in OK?" he asks as he places the mugs on coasters.

"It's been four days now," I tell him.

"Not long. I was sad when I heard the news. When your child dies it's sad even when you know you'll see them again."

"I'll need to visit mum soon," I say. "I've messaged her."

"Yeah, you'll have a lot of people to visit. Just keep in touch with people so they don't worry about you," he advises me.

"Yeah I will."

After we drink the tea, Dad shows me around the house. It's a large four-bedroom property with one acre of land. He's grown vegetables in his garden. There're potatoes and carrots growing in large numbers.

He tells me how he has hired help to tend his huge garden. How he's befriended someone who he pays a good rate of digi-currency to work for him a couple of times a week, helping with the gardening.

We talk often on Watts-app and once in a while I visit him via hologram. I've seen his house before but it's different actually being here. Smelling the scene of the natural cleaning products he's used and looking at how he's made his mark on his new home.

He asks me about my funeral. I tell him it will be taking place at the beginning of next month but how I didn't want to view any recordings. I asked for it to be held at Emmanuel church where I attended since my mid-twenties.

We gossip about this world. He tells me about a recent day adventure he went on when he visited the Grand Canyon of second phase. He took a load of pictures and videos. He went to an American diner nearby that was geared for tourists and ordered a meal. He said that had been enough for him and then he teleported home.

That's so him! When he was alive, we would arrange weekend trips via Ryan Air and fly to European cities for extra short vacations. We would have a few meals, buy a few little trinkets in the city and then be gone a day later. That's the way he enjoyed his holidays. We would take these little breaks every few years.

My dad made more tea and brought out some Mr Kipling cakes. We talked about my grand-children.

"Do you want to stay over here today?" Dad asks.

"Yeah, if that's OK?"

My dad assures me that it's fine. He shows me the three spare bedrooms and asks me which one I'd like to have. I pick the middle one in the house upstairs, it's a good size room. The room is empty apart from the grey carpet.

"What sort of furniture should I download? Do you want me to do it now as it takes about half an hour to materialize," my dad asks.

Dad lets me pick what I want. I choose a single brown bed and flowery bedding. I buy a small TV stand and a television. I had a small TV at home when I lived with dad. He buys me a games console and shows me how to copy my laptop so that a copy will be registered to my room here. We have to fill out some forms that I consent for this. It says the computer will take a day to process. All the other bits will be ready within half an hour.

I see an outline of the furniture in the room after he has paid. It's just white dots in the shape of a TV and a bed. We watch for a minute as they begin to colour and blur into being. It will take a little while before they are solid. We will receive an email alert when the furnishings are completely downloaded and belong to us.

*

"I was reading in the newspaper about the levels of war and how it has decreased almost completely since second phase was introduced," Dad says.

"I know, the world is moving in leaps and bounds."

Dad's phone beeps and he lets me know that my room's furniture has downloaded.

"The room's looking smart," Dad says as we look around the bedroom.

The walls are bare of artwork so I think I'd like to buy some pictures when my computer downloads a copy tomorrow. The two-bed sofa sits by the window and the yellow curtains let in a little light that gently illuminates the room in a soft glow.

"Do you want anything to eat?"

"Um, maybe later. I had cake and tea just a while ago," I admit.

Dad leaves me to get accustomed to the room. He's bought me a little 20-inch television that fits on a table above my bed. There is a stripy armchair next to my bed so I can watch films and play my Xbox.

I had an older model of Xbox in the world as when I grew older I played video games a lot less and tended to just use it to watch films. This is the latest model and it looks impressive. I am easily able to sign into my account and all the films and video games I've purchased since my teens are there.

I've been playing Xbox before the twelfth model came out. I remember receiving it when I was fourteen. My mum got it for me from Argos.

My new console has apps, which allow me to connect to my communication in Second Life as well as Earth. The console's data is aware that I now belong to second phase.

I like my room and feel at home. I sit on the armchair and look around. It's so nice that my dad is letting me have a home from home at his house. It makes me feel like a young woman again when I would stay at his house when I became lonely. I would often visit him if I hadn't had much company from friends during the week.

I check my phone and look at the shopping apps that I have on it. I still have amazon. My card details have changed to digi currency and I'm no longer logged into amazon.co.uk but amazon.2NDPhase.x. It still has all the books and films I bought in life on my account.

I know what I want to buy and I can't wait to see it in front of me. I order Blueray copies of Buffy the Vampire Slayer the complete boxset. I click pay and laugh at how cheap it is in this digital currency. I own the films on my digital collection, but I want them on Blueray like I have in the home I shared with Casper.

I remember when I was a teenager and lived with mum in Aylesbury, I had a special edition Blueray copy of this show. I remember watching the discs with a friend called Cherry who was my best friend at the time and also loved the show. The show was a hit from over a hundred years ago, yet it was still popular.

I call my mum's mobile. She doesn't answer at first. I'd spoken to her briefly on Watts-app but hadn't really been able to talk about what I was going through in depth and I'd expressed that I needed time before I really chatted with family. She understood, it's not like there was a shortage of time here.

Mum calls me back a few minutes later. I feel my hand shake as I answer. "Hi, Mum."

"Croc croc," she says, which had always been our joke greeting after it was how we described the mannerisms of a dog we had when I was in my late twenties.

"Croc, I'm okay. Goodness there's so much to discuss. Have you spoken to my girls since I entered here?"

"Miranda called me, she was really upset and visited me via hologram. I've chatted a little with Eliza too."

It made me sad to think of my daughter's sadness because I was no longer around to visit in person. "Eliza's sorting out my funeral soon. I've left her a small budget. You know me, didn't want to spend a lot on something like that."

"Don't blame you. Your memory will live on and you don't need to tap into a lot of money to achieve this." Mum sounds young on the phone.

She had rejuvenated to her appearance in her twenties. I never realized that she was quite a beautiful young person before my time really. She had me at twenty-one so I was too young to remember her as a young woman, although I remember she had long dark hair.

"Would you like to visit me and dad? We're at his house," I say.

"Yes, I am meant to go on a trek with a friend tomorrow so I won't be able to stay too long. I could visit for lunch and go by seven. Would that be okay?"

Mum would often go on horse treks. No animals were brought over to second phase so all the creatures that you saw were programs and thus never behaved out of sync.

When Mum arrives at Dad's house, she is dressed in a long checked dress, her hair is long and loose with a fringe.

"She's made herself at home here," Dad tells her, showing her my new room in his house.

"It's like when she was young and lived with you the last two years of her university years," Mum says.

I had taken five years to complete a three-year bachelor's degree. I experienced severe ill health in the form of schizo-effective disorder which is basically a combination of bipolar and schizophrenia.

Modern medicine had improved so much that I was only in hospital for two weeks with psychosis when I was twenty-three. I was given a special medication that quelled the psychosis quickly.

I would hear voices that I believed were people I knew talking to me through the television. My speech became scrambled and obscene at times.

I entered a psychiatric ward in Aylesbury and returned to my studies the following academic year. Even though I recovered from psychosis within two weeks, I was ordered to stay there for three months to recover. The hospital was very pleasant with a lot of activities such as a gym and art studio.

My dad had always been helpful to me when I lived with him and moved in for my studies. I had lived with him during the last two years of my bachelor's degree.

He would make me nice meals and help me out with money when I needed it. He helped me sort out claim for a benefit called DPLA which was introduced in 2200's all around the country. DPLA gave a person who didn't work and were classified disabled, fifteen thousand pounds a year in benefits – the national minimum wage for forty hours a week was twenty thousand. I would eventually go back to work but remained on this benefit for a few years.

"Shall I make us all a cup of tea," Dad says.

"Please," Mum replies.

I smile to myself because all the Bluerays I've ordered have downloaded. I will organize them on the shelf. I think a bedroom needs Bluerays.

Mum died only a few years ago. She was always a very active and healthy woman. She did horse riding and dog walking. She had a vegan diet. I remember feeling so blue when she had passed away, knowing both my parents were gone from the real world.

I sit down on the sofa and Mum takes a seat on Dad's armchair. I tell her to pick another seat as he likes to sit there. Dad comes back shortly with more tea and plates of sandwiches.

One of his ways of caring for people is making them nice food. He trained as an apprentice chef for part of his life and makes wonderful food. I'll be glad to enjoy his cooking again.

"I like how you've decorated the place," Mum says to Dad.

"Thanks. Some of the paintings aren't mine. I like supporting artists around the world for their gifts. The one's that aren't mine are all from artists in the real world, prints of course."

Mum and I talk about many different things. She said she'd like to teach me to horse ride in Utopia. Utopia is the name of the city in the imagined world that she lives in. There was no danger of injury in this existence.

I agreed that it would be nice to learn something new. Mum didn't want to stay for dinner so, when she left to go home, Dad made fish and chips. As in life, his portions were grand.

"Food good?" Dad asks.

"Hold on one sec, I'm just going to take a photograph for my Instagram," I say and click.

I tell Dad that my funeral is taking place next month at Emmanuel church in Chesham.

One thing important to clarify when describing my life in second phase, and all the people who live in it; is that you can still choose to die. I was forty when the program was shown to the world and the technology was like something from a science fiction movie.

Your chip is what keeps you alive. Copies are stored around the world. Your consciousness can never be deleted from these chips that are stored on the second phase database.

Yet, if a person tires of this life, for whatever reason, and truly wants to die in the way nature intended, then they have to first go through a procedure that will mean their chips are deleted. All their data and information on how they lived in second phase will still be on record but it will be archived for future researchers to look at.

To die like this, you have to go through a lot of psychological assessments and sign a lot of legal papers. I've heard of people on talk shows expressing how they are now ready to die. Explaining how the last years they've had in second phase have been enough. People often express a desire to meet with family who died before second phase existed, or to be with God.

After dinner, I tell Dad that I'm going to go to my room. He touches my arm and his hand feels solid. "Okay. See you in the morning," he says with a smile.

"Night, Dad," I say and make my way upstairs.

I put a Buffy Blueray in the Xbox. I curl up and start watching season one. It takes me back to a place of comfort.

*

Chapter six

Over the rest of the week I call up Casper. We talk for hours and he tells me how little Snowball is missing me. It makes me weep. He tells me how Eliza is contacting the solicitor to help with the arrangement of my earthly assets. I'm pleased as it is something that is really important to me.

When Casper comes to see me in my own home via hologram he looks tired. I tell him to make sure he eats properly.

We sit on the sofa and watch a TV channel from the real world. It is a mundane exercise but we were old people and it is comforting. We watch 'This morning' on ITV, which had been on television for hundreds of years.

The current presenters were a pretty red-headed woman and a portly, homely-looking man. They were a pleasure to watch and we laughed at the funny topic of one of their pieces where they compared the price of cheap and expensive pants.

"Pants!" laughs Casper.

We laugh together at his remark and spend a good while together just talking. Talking about us and what we would do when it was his time in this world. He wants his house to be sold and the money to be split between our daughters. But in second phase he expresses how he doesn't want to live here in Chesham. He wants to explore countries of the printed world he never got to see in life. What he wants to do is become young and travel.

"We could even renew our wedding vows when I come over to your side," he suggests.

"That would be a beautiful idea."

That night Casper signs off from the hologram just before I go to sleep. Tomorrow was Tuesday, which meant it would be a day I spend with my guide, Emily.

*

Emily arrives at the time we arranged which is twelve noon. I need my beauty sleep, I guess. I've downloaded lots of lovely new clothes and I greet her in a floral dress.

She's wearing low cut brown trousers and a florescent green top with a black cardigan over it. Her hair is tied up high. She looks young and fresh.

"How has your week been?" Emily says.

I tell her about meeting with my parents. How I've caught up with my husband by the holographic services. I tell her how he wants to travel when it's his time to get here. He wants to see all the places in the world that he couldn't afford to visit in life.

"That's great. You're doing so well here," Emily says.

"I've got the company of all my family. I was anxious to call my daughters but I got around to it, eventually. Miranda seems to be taking it the hardest that I've passed. She cried on the phone," I tell her.

"Bless her. It's not easy, I know. Do your daughters live locally to where you lived in Chesham?"

"My daughters all live in different locations around London. All were easy enough to get to," I say.

"That's good. It's nice to be able to visit family."

Emily tells me how today's session will introduce me to activities that I can take up in second phase. I can look into work and hobbies. I can teleport anywhere that I am granted access to via my watch, so I'm not bound to a location the way one would be in the real world. I could take art classes in Alabama if I chose to!

"You've only been here a week. No one expects you to want to get working just yet. But your time, though it stretches out for the unimaginable foreseeable future, is precious. What were your interests when you were alive? I remember from our last meeting what a good voice you had," Emily says.

"Yes. I adored singing all through my life. As I got older my voice was less powerful and even here my body reflects that. I'm not ready to get younger yet. It doesn't seem right until Casper joins me, which I hope is a long time away. He's also ninety, his birthday's a month after mine, but I'd be thrilled to see him reach a hundred years of age."

"You're a lovely wife by the sounds of it." Emily's smile is warm. "What is Casper like?"

"Well, he's an artist – a wonderful painter. Very technical but also imaginative. He's been a vegetarian since I met him. He's quite a reserved person but very interesting to talk to."

"He sounds lovely." Emily gets out her tablet from her backpack. "Today we are going to set you some occupations – if you wish to that is. I have one session with you a week, so I can accompany you to events for support."

"I'd like to do more karaoke," I say. I can remember all the amazing memories of singing in my life.

"More karaoke sounds fun. We could go back to the bar you sang in last week. Hey, what about joining a karaoke club?"

I have many memories of singing in my life. When I was in middle school I sung in the playground in front of my peers. They would prompt me to sing after first hearing me. I still remember a girl I thought thoroughly horrible said she thought I'd be famous because of my singing voice.

"Oh, I can't tell you how much I'd love that. I have been singing in choirs and at karaoke all throughout my life. I've sung in America in karaoke booths and on apps. It's always been an important part of my life," I say, feeling excited.

"I'm glad I was assigned to work with you, you're an interesting character, Jessica."

I make myself a cup of tea as Emily sits down in my living room. She compliments how I've decorated it, making it lovely and homely. We decide that we will go to the Fladh in the imagined world for now. I express how I want to get to know people there and build a bit of a social life around that karaoke bar.

I show her my karaoke apps on my phone with recordings I made in life. I show her my Soundcloud as well which has recordings from when I had my last singing lesson aged twenty-six. I didn't want another teacher after that as I was really happy with my voice and felt my sound was unique. I was more interested in pop music than opera.

Emily downloads the karaoke app that I have and follows me. I have a lot of followers on one of them downloaded when I was thirty. That was the age I first met Casper.

*

Emily and I go back to Nilba, the picturesque town in the imagined world. The pink sky is dreamy and the soft white sand feels good against my shoes. It is a warm day and there is a calm feeling in this place.

Emily and I go back to the Fladh where I sang last week. We are greeted by the black man who runs the place. He introduced himself last time as Dave. When we enter the bar, he waves and smiles at us.

"Good to see you again," Dave says. "What do you think you'll sing this time?"

"I love the song 'Tattooed' that Maxeen Bandana sang," I say.

"Okay. We've got all the songs here. So that's not a problem." Dave types the name of the song into his karaoke app on his tablet.

"Has it been busy in here?" I ask.

"It's never that busy if I'm honest. We're a small community of singers. But we have a good few characters enter, mostly regulars."

"Well I like it in here," I say.

"I'll give you a shout when the singing starts," Dave tells me.

Emily and I find a seat near the front of the Irish-themed bar. I get myself a cherry daquiri, it only has a little alcohol and I don't plan to have another one tonight. As I have the constitution of an old lady, the drink warms my spirits and makes me feel the cool calm of a tipple.

"Nice drink?" Emily asks.

"Yes, I've never been much of a drinker. Did you know I had health problems in my life?"

"Yes, I read your basic records when I was assigned to you, all the things that were available to be disclosed to healthcare professionals working with you on second phase. I read how you had an episode when you were at university.

"Thank you, it wasn't always easy. I talked to my daughters and said if they ever got sick to see about the cure, but thankfully none of them have inherited it. I see the cure working all around the world for mental illnesses caused by neurological imbalances. All the other 'cure' pills that quell conditions such as anxiety and depression. It's just another way science has saved this world again and again."

"Quite right, science rocks," Emily responds.

"It's the most amazing thing that we have on this Earth. That and faith."

Emily just smiles. A short silence falls on our table and then Dave announces that the karaoke will start. There aren't many people in the Fladh today. There's got to be less than ten customers filling up this big bar. Dave is dealing with the karaoke and there's a woman serving behind the bar.

The first singer that performs is a man that is dressed very modern. His fashion is from a movement that started about five years ago. Emily wears a lot of the same of florescent colouring, but I guess she dulls it down for work. He has florescent green hair that is long and curled and his make-up is covers his face in patches of colour.

The man sings an operatic song extremely well. The crowd watch and are welcoming of the performance. After his performance he tells us he died in his twenties but that he feels alive. I feel sad for him but so glad that second phase exists – no one ever needs to die, not truly.

When it's my turn to sing I perform, 'tattooed' by Maxeen Bandana. I remember singing this song accompanied with piano with a vocal coach who lived in Dolis Hill in London. I would take the tube to get there. I really enjoyed the lessons because we would record the performances for me to upload online.

I did my best and the crowd were positive and receptive as they had been with the young man with florescent green hair. After my performance I feel my heart fluttering in my chest and I enjoy the sense of adrenalin that this induces.

Emily and I talk some more. I order a small Diet Coke and we listen to the singers. Not all of them are great but the atmosphere is good. I sing a soft rock song next which was by an obscure band that I knew from the internet, yet the Fladh karaoke has available all the songs that are on Spotify.

When the evening is over, I go to say goodbye to Dave, wanting to make his acquaintance. I plan to bring some of my old friends who have died and live in second phase to this bar.

"Can I have a word with you before you leave?" Dave says.

"Of course, we're in no rush," I say, smiling at him and Emily who stands by my side.

"Well, I run a small recording studio down the road. I ask all the good singers, and even the not so good singers who seem to be regulars, if they would like to record a single. But I would like to help the better singers more, as it's a joy to work with talented vocalists. I'd love to record a track with you."

I agree at once. I never got the chance to record music for Spotify in my life. I tell Dave about how I was in a metal band in Buckinghamshire when I was seventeen. He tells me how he lived in Wembley for some time, but spent part of his childhood in the Caribbean.

We exchange phone numbers and arrange a date next week to work on a song that I will record for a debut single. He explains that animations are so accessible in modern times, especially in second phase that I could even make a music video. He's not giving these services away for free, but, like everything in second phase, the fee is nominal.

He explains to me how if I want I can either choose to make the profits in real world currency or second phase money. I tell him that I have a lot of funds for my life in second phase already.

"I suggest you make it real life money then. Do you have children? It could benefit them."

I tell him briefly about my three girls. The karaoke is about to resume, so he tells me to call him and arrange a date of recording. He writes down a link for me to look at his website to see all the packages available.

*

I spend the rest of the day at home with Emily looking into the types of volunteering that I can do.

Emily is excited about Dave's proposition and we browse his web page on my laptop. It shows how he works not only in the Fladh, but other karaoke bars in the imagined world of Freedom.

He gives a bio of himself and there are pictures of him. His website talks about how he is a music producer and how he worked at this as a side line in his life. When he entered second phase, five years ago this became his main job. He died due to heart complications according to his webpage bio.

"The album production is so cheap for your budget," squeaks Emily in excitement.

"I know. It's like the cost of a few toiletries would have been on Earth," I state, marvelling, not for the first time, the exchange rate of digi currency.

"Yes, and I think people would warm to you," Emily says.

"I will book this," I say, feeling so excited.

Emily makes me a cup of tea and places it down on my coffee table. She sits next to me as I book a production of an EP, which is four songs. Which, like I said is about the price of cheap shampoo and set in the real world. I am excited, as I confirm how I want the money from the profits to be paid in real world currency. When my tracks are finalized, they will be produced through SoundHouse, and be available on Spotify and other digital mediums in both this world and the real world.

I touch my debit card against the laptop screen. My payment confirms the session, which is booked for when I next see Emily the following week. I feel excited beyond words. Emily expresses how it's great to support me in such a great project. Her managers are pleased with the progress I am making.

Emily hugs me goodbye before she leaves. It unnerves me a little as of course, she has no substance being only a hologram.

I drink my tea and think about the day. I had done something amazing. I sang in front of a positive and vibrant crowd of people and booked the production of my first ever studio EP. I couldn't wait to tell friends and family.

*

A day later my family pop round. Their holographic selves feel as real as my guide does. The technology is wonderful and means that I don't have to miss them while they live their lives without me in the real world.

My husband Casper arrives first and comments on how the house looks so homely.

"I'm going to redecorate soon", he says as he embraces me. His hair seems to have thinned and it seems whiter than I recall.

We chat about what he's going to do with our home in the real world. He wants to make it vibrant and full of art. He says that his friends think he should let an interior designer revamp the place.

"But they're expensive!" I exclaim.

"Oh, no, they're students from Bucks New University. They'd be doing it for free. There's a young girl in our church who's starting a degree in interior design."

"Well, free is a fine price. If it makes you happy to change the appearance of things, a change can always be good," I say.

Casper asks me about my life here in second phase. He's really excited about the EP of covers that I am producing which will be available on all digital platforms in both this world and the real world.

"My beautiful wife. You've always been such a wonderful singer," he says, his brown eyes so warm and kind.

I simply blush and tell him what songs I've picked.

We have an hour before our daughters are due to visit. The grandchildren aren't visiting for a while. Miranda and Kate's children are finding it difficult to deal with my passing. I've seen how family in general have expressed my death on Facebook. I haven't commented on those things as I felt it would be distasteful.

When you die, your Facebook goes green – if you enter second phase that is. If you choose to move on to the spirit world and not become digitized, like traditional death, Facebook either close your account or make it a memorial page. If they keep it open to be managed by a close family or friend, it becomes a navy blue as opposed to a light blue colour of a person alive in the world.

This happens for other social media too. I love looking at Instagram and seeing the pictures of my family and friends.

"How's doggy?" I ask.

"Oh, she's fine. I got her some new luxury dog food from Waitrose the other day," Casper says.

Casper and I walk around the house. He says that he loves how it's the same as it was years ago and how it's a good way to adjust slowly to second phase.

Casper perches on the double bed and strokes the flowery bed cover. Of course, he can't feel its velvety texture, the way I can.

"Do you want me to tell the people at church about your EP?" Casper smiles.

"Sure. Dave, the man who's producing my EP will be posting on his social media about the project throughout production and once it's released." I beam.

"I remember all the covers you did. How you sung karaoke in all those pubs. I was always mesmerized by your beautiful singing. You've always had a unique voice. It's one of the things that I love about you," Casper says.

*

Eliza is the first to arrive of my girls. She's wearing an orange pencil dress and black cardigan. She has her long brown hair tied in a high ponytail.

"Wow, mum, you look just like you did the other day. Goodness, it takes my breath away," Eliza exclaims.

"I've missed you," I say, not meaning to say it, but not being able to stop myself.

"Me too," she smiles, "but you're not gone from life. I'll join you in that digital world one day when I'm old like you. But I think I'll restore myself to the appearance of my twenties immediately."

Eliza sits herself on the flowery sofa. She asks about the singing that her father has been so proud of. Eliza kept up her singing lessons until she became a professional singing teacher herself. She always enjoyed classical music.

When they were young, I taught them the basic vocal scales. I couldn't play the piano, so I used a program that played the piano on my tablet. We had various vocal training Bluerays in the house. When each of my girls reached six, they had lessons with a local teacher.

"Kate messaged me on Facebook. She can't make it. But she's really excited about your EP," Eliza says.

"OK. No problem. There's always another time," I say.

Eliza tells me how Mariah is finishing her BTEC in dance this year. She's planning on taking a gap year to work full time before studying dance at uni. Mariah looks like her mum when she was that age except she's coloured her hair a golden blond. It really suits her.

Miranda arrives shortly after and then everyone is here. Eliza tells me Kate will visit next time. It will be good to see Mariah and Miranda's children soon but for now they need to get on with their lives and not think about second phase.

"Mariah can come visit when she's finished her BTEC. I'm gonna let Kate know Megan and Kaleb can visit when they've finished college too," I say.

"I'll let Kate know," Eliza says. "I know Kaleb's finished his studies. He's got the year off."

"Well, let's give it till after I've recorded my EP."

We talk about a lot of different things before going for a walk in the town. We go to the park. The only animals are visual recordings, which aren't sentient beings, just like photographs really, to remind people in this world of the beauty of animals.

In the park Eliza nudges Miranda.

"Not now," Miranda says, shaking her head.

"It's exciting," Eliza almost shouts.

"It's scary more like," Miranda whispers.

"What are you two on about?" I say, feeling concerned.

Miranda confesses to me the news she had been anxious to tell me. She and her partner Ashley want to have a baby, but they were musing the more modern way to conceive.

"Did the doctor say you'd experience problems having a baby the traditional way?" I say.

"I don't know. I didn't even ask my doctor that. I just told them my weight and how I wanted a baby. I knew that I'd get the treatment free on the NHS."

Miranda wears size eighteen jeans but told me how she's eighteen stone since her last weigh in. If one's BMI is over normal, you can qualify to have a baby through the 'modern womb'.

All it means is that your partners sperm and a female's eggs are put in an artificial machine that grows the baby. It was one of the scientific advancements that came about the same time of the development of second phase.

I was young then and at the time it wasn't on the NHS. I'm glad I carried my three girls but I felt that this would be a wonderful thing for Miranda.

"Beckton's a nice place. Quiet but so close to central London. We don't know if we will move. But the idea is to get the treatment around next summer. With the rent from the inherited house, we can get a mortgage easily. But first were going to have the baby and then make a life plan."

"You enjoy your job," I remark.

"Yeah, true. I love getting to design things. Ashley's happy too."

We talk about ideas for baby names. Miranda wants something modern and original for a name. Once the baby is ready to pick up at the hospital, she tells me how she'll look up the perfect original name for the boy or girl. She tells me how she's bought a book called 'Funky baby names'.

After returning from our walk, the girls make to leave. Eliza tells me how she's planning to visit her sister Miranda soon and go shopping. "Charity shops will be visited," she huffs.

Casper stays for a little while longer. We watch The X-Factor together. I remember how in my late twenties I started watching it religiously.

"I better go and get doggy's dinner," Casper says eventually. "I'll visit you tomorrow if you like?"

When Casper is gone and I am alone, I look up the hospital in Newham, which is the London Borough where Miranda will be growing her baby.

I've seen documentaries of how it's done. Miranda and her partner Ashley have already given their sperm and eggs so that the child will be one hundred percent theirs. Their specimens are now frozen until the nine-month process will take place. The artificial wombs are very efficient and the same size as a woman's womb would be.

They look all weird in their grey sacks of fluids and artificial heart but they completely grow a baby without having to physically carry it. Miranda tells me how in her late thirties she had some of her eggs frozen and I'm really excited for her.

I look up the building online. It's a very old-fashioned building but has all the modern science a hospital could need.

*

Tomorrow I would have a guide session with Emily, where I would look at what I wanted to do in my life. I had a leaflet, which showed how I was more able to change endeavours in second phase than I ever could have been in real life.

I wanted to work within second phase. I had only been dead less than a month and revived in the digital world. My family were only just getting used to my passing. Death has never been the same since the digital creation of this world. For everyone that enters is existing as fully as they do in the world.

I firmly believe in God. I have been a Christian all my life. The church family that I attended in Chesham had mixed opinions about second phase. A lot of people had expressed that eventually they would traditionally die in second phase and enter real death.

When you die in second phase, you must sign certain legal papers that mean your data will become unconscious and the science that keeps you alive in a digital existence will let your essence die and return to whatever realm lies beyond human death.

I think I will want this for myself one day. I want to maybe live a thousand years in second phase. Scientists have found planets which they believe will allow humans and other creatures to inhabit. I want to be able to hear about that in the news.

I am excited for my life in this realm. Today is one of those special days. I'm to visit the Fladh this afternoon and record my EP with Dave.

*

It's 1 pm when I get there. I love being able to teleport to this place in the imagined worlds. Dave is waiting for me at the bar. He's drinking a coffee and smiles when he sees me.

The pub is empty apart from the lady who works behind the bar and Dave. They are playing quiet music in the background.

"Have you had a good weekend?" Dave asks me.

"Yes, thank you. I had family over."

"Oh, good. I'm seeing my daughter on Wednesday. She always visits on a Wednesday as it's her day off work," Dave tells me.

I had seen photographs of his daughter on his Instagram. She was a woman in her fifties in the real world.

Dave shows me to the recording studio. He waves goodbye to the bar lady and we walk down the beach to his home where the recording studio is in his spare room. His flat is in a modern white complex. It is a small two-bedroom apartment, with the larger of the bedrooms converted for his music.

I've been practising my songs on my phone. I've chosen 'Tattooed' by Maxeen Bandana, as I remember singing that with my final vocal coach in my late twenties. I hadn't wanted any more singing lessons as I loved the sound I had and didn't want lessons to change the voice I'd found.

The second song we choose is an original that I had written in my life. It's called 'Caught in the Middle'. Dave had been so quick in preparing the backing track and sending it to me. I was thrilled to think this would be available on all digital music platforms soon.

The two final songs were covers. One was of a Bekki song I always loved called 'Heavenly', and the last song was one that Dave had picked.

I did a few scales with Dave who played his keyboard. After five minutes we started with the first song – 'Tattooed'. We recorded this one with a piano backing track. Dave was an average pianist and the recording wasn't by him but by a site that charged for backing tracks. It was all legit to use them on albums for consumption.

I loved singing this. The song requires softness and power at different moments. I remembered myself, that chubby girl in her late twenties singing this with my vocal coach in Dolis Hill in London. I remember having a lot of respect for him and feeling he was a really decent coach. I remembered these moments as I sang. My voice was that of my age, ninety years old, but it was still a powerful vocal.

Dave had used his music software to add a jazz production to the backing track. It set my heart alight.

The final two songs had similar backing tracks to the original pop productions by the artists. When the recordings were all completed and we were happy with the recordings, Dave begun to master them.

I sat on the blue sofa behind his studio equipment watching as he began editing the pitch and wave file.

"I always love this moment, the anticipation of it all," Dave told me.

"When will it be available for the world?"

"Well this bit will take me a while. I'll be ready in about an hour or two to send it to SoundHouse. I always use them to produce my albums."

As Dave worked his magic with the EP production, we chatted. He told me about all the artists and bands he'd worked with in SecondPhase. He loved how cheap it was to produce music in this world.

"In my twenty years since death, I've worked with hundreds of artists," he said. His artist page on Facebook had fifty-thousand likes.

We took a selfie together for the social media. There I was an old lady with long grey hair and glasses. He was a man who had died of a sudden heart attack. Everyone who opts for SecondPhase has a chip in their neck, which means if they die unexpectedly, they'll be uploaded to this wonderful digital world. That's exactly what happened with Dave.

He's a tall black man with no hair and a kind calm face. He's wearing a white jumper and I'm wearing a snazzy rockabilly dress and cardigan in the photo. He posts the picture and writes how my EP is on its way on the Facebook page.

"It's been a joy to produce an EP with you Jessica," he says while typing on his music program on the Imac in front of him. "If you ever want to produce an album, I'd be happy to but let's try and get some buzz about this first. My rates go up for album production but it's pittance isn't it, on our end?"

When the album is produced and finalized on SoundHouse, it is in a huge queue but Dave assures me it will only take a couple of days before it is on all the digital platforms.

    We go back to the Fladh to celebrate the EP being on its way. I get talking to some of the people attending karaoke that day. It's around six pm when we get there. Karaoke hasn't begun yet and the pub is serving meals. We order food and sing later that evening.

    I choose a country music song that I remember singing on holiday the first time I went to the USA, aged twenty-six. I chose to go to Nashville because I thought it seemed an interesting city. I sung that song in a karaoke booth in the main mall called Opray Mills.

    I stayed out late that evening and got a lot of new twitter contacts and made acquaintance of other singers. Some were elderly but didn't look it due to rejuvenating their appearance. I was a rarity in Second Phase. Most people wanted to be back in their most glamorous years. I was sure that I would wait till Casper joined me for that.

    I left the pub at eleven at night, teleporting out on my watch. Returning home, I made myself a cup of hot chocolate.

    I texted Casper and other family members good night and messaged my parents to let them know the EP production had gone well.

*

One year passed. My EP received a lot of positive comments on social media from Dave's facebook page. A lot of people streamed the music and I grew a small following on social media as a musician.

    At the same time, I visit my mum in the imagined worlds. We went on holiday together to a magical hippy city for a couple of weeks. It was like a fairy tale how peaceful and beautiful the city was. In life we had often gone on holiday together.

Miranda had her baby through the modern method. The baby grew in the fertility box at the hospital and she came to the hospital weekly to see how her child was growing. She had a beautiful boy who she named Henry.

My children all had their inheritance. I had left one of my daughters my home which I bought in life. I had been lucky enough that both dad and mum left me a home and I had been able to pass one on to each of my remaining daughters. My family had been made very comfortable from my inheritance and that was a true blessing to be able to endow.

Since Second Phase has become reality, the world has slowly become a more socially just place. War has been eradicated through political advancements and fairer foreign policy.

Britain has become a place where even those who don't work receive thirteen thousand pounds a year to live on if a single person and up to twenty-six for a couple.

Education is free for a first degree but costs three thousand a year if people choose to study equivalent qualifications.

I have a new grandson who will visit me when old enough through holograms until his own death many, many years in the future. I love seeing his photos on Facebook and Instagram, it makes my heart happy.

Casper has urged me to reinvent myself for the production of my album. He says he wanted to see a picture on the cover of how I looked at thirty. So, I agreed to the painless procedure and now look like a young woman. I chose to be averagely slim instead of slightly overweight, like I had actually been in my thirties.

I had always been pretty and it makes me feel confident. I am glad that Casper urged me to make the change. I went to a local salon and got my hair cut. I kept it the dark brown I had in my life. I had a new fringe and some layers added to make myself a little different.

I wrote ten original songs for the album. Dave helped a lot and we had a blast producing it. We recorded two music videos and had an animator produce one. All at such cheap costs. My EP was doing well and my following was anticipating the new album with a much younger-looking me.

In the real world, Casper is doing well. He is going on holiday with our daughter Eliza to Paris and is very excited about the trip.

I am a new woman. I've finished my guide sessions with Emily and I sent her an Itunes gift card to thank her for all her kind help in getting me adjusted to this reality.

I have a fan base and my musical life has evolved. I am not famous or anything, but I have fans in the real world as well as Second Phase. I make a little money on my music, which is given to my grandchildren through royalties.

I will soon be touring places in Second Phase performing concerts. My voice sounds youthful in the album compared to the EP where my voice had been that of an old lady. I am a pretty woman who still has the mind of an old grandmother.

My family attends the occasional gig as holographic members. They have their own lives to live.

I plan to keep going with music and do other amazing things during my time in Second Phase. I want to stay here for at least a thousand years. I am in love with life.

Printed in Great Britain
by Amazon

38814414R00038